GOOD BABIES

A Tale of Trolls, Humans, a Witch, and a Switch

Tim Myers   illustrated by Kelly Murphy

CANDLEWICK PRESS
CAMBRIDGE, MASSACHUSETTS

ong ago a family had a farm in a valley deep in the mountains of Norway. There they worked hard and were happy. But after a third child was born to them, things were not so rosy. This baby slept all day, cried all night, and drove everyone crazy, no matter how they rocked him or sang to him or made funny faces.

But things were no better for the troll-family nearby. They loved the thick forests and boulder-strewn heights of the mountains, especially their dank, spacious cavern. But they had a new baby too, and he was a terror, sleeping all night when the family was awake and crying all day, which is when trolls take to their beds. And not even a treat like fresh eagle-droppings would calm him so his family could rest.

One summer twilight a dark-eyed witch, coming from beyond the lands of the Lapps and the Finns, was traveling along the valley on some evil errand to the south. She had ears so magically sharp they could catch the padding of mice feet in a shut barn, or the swimming of seals beneath sea ice. So when she heard the wailing of two babies, one from the valley and one from the high, pine-covered ridges, she got an idea.

Ah, she told herself, two families, human and troll, each with a new brat. What a wonderful chance to refresh my travel-weary bones with some wickedness. I'll just *switch* the babies!

So when midnight came, she crept to the farmhouse window, lifted the human baby out, and carried it away. Since her nose was keen too, she had no trouble finding the trolls' cavern up in the mountains.

And there, before anyone could see, she sneaked in, put the human baby in the troll's stony cradle, and stole the troll-baby away. Then she hurried back down to the valley to leave the troll-baby at the farmhouse.

A troll-baby living with humans? A human baby with trolls? What chaos and heartache that would lead to! Cackling gleefully in the moonlight, the witch went on her way.

The farm family woke up refreshed the next morning, surprised and relieved that their baby had slept through the night.

In the days that followed, though, the baby began acting strangely.

Though he slept when he was supposed to, he would sometimes crawl outside to bathe in a mud puddle, or pull the cat's tail just to hear it yowl. He loved to chew on rocks and straw—and he was growing quite strong. And although the mother wouldn't hear of it, the rest of the family thought he was getting uglier and uglier.

When he picked up the cow and his father yelled at him to put it down, he just laughed—and the farmer lost his patience. "What shall we do with this child!" he roared.

"Love him till he learns better," said the wife.

The farmer grew quiet. "You're right," he said.

Up in their cavern, the troll family was having trouble too. Their trollkin now slept by day, but he was oddly pale and smooth-faced.

When he cooed and babbled, it sounded strange to his parents—like the murmuring of a brook or the trilling of a bird. He wouldn't play with bones or swamp-sod like his brothers and sisters did. Instead, if he saw a bit of sunlight shining under the great stone door, he'd try to pick it up. And although the troll-mother wouldn't hear of it, the rest of the family thought he was getting uglier and uglier.

One day he dumped out a perfectly delicious bowl of earthworm soup—and when his father yelled at him, he just giggled. The whole family stood around him, tearing their matted hair. "He's a bad baby!" the troll-brats screeched.

"Then we must be patient and kind, and teach him," said the hideous, soft-eyed wife.

"Yes, Mama," said the troll-brats.

As weeks went by, things got even worse. Now the farm family's baby started waking up at night again—which would have been wonderful for trolls but left the humans all red-eyed and grumpy.

And up in the mountain cavern, the trolls' baby began waking up during the day. The trolls' eyes got puffy and blue, and they started grinding their teeth and saying terrible things to each other.

One evening, however, the dark-eyed witch passed the farmhouse again, on the way home to her ice fortress on Svalbard. So she peeked in at the window to see how her scheme was working.

In the bright kitchen, the farm wife was feeding her baby, who'd grown so big he hardly fit in his highchair. "Why won't you eat?" the human mother was saying piteously. "This is *kremkake*—cream cake—and with strawberries! You're just being stubborn!"

But then the sound of a lullaby came to the witch. The farm wife had taken the knobby, rough-skinned baby from the highchair and now sat with him in her lap, singing in warm, low tones—and his yellowish eyes were closed in happiness as he snuggled in her arms.

Straining her ears, the witch could hear from far off a troll-mother's lullaby too, drifting down in snatches with the wind from the mountains—and she knew the troll-mother was rocking her own strange baby.

Well! If the two families were now happy with their babies, she could easily take care of that! She'd switch them back! Bristling with rage, she waited till the farm wife had laid her baby in the cradle for the night, and again she stole him away.

Then she climbed through the forested slopes to the troll cavern. The trolls were all out looking for something disgusting for their new child—berries or eggs or apples—since he wouldn't touch the rotten badger meat they'd had for dinner. It was a simple matter to leave the troll-baby there and carry the human baby back to his true family.

"That will fix them!" the witch muttered in angry satisfaction as she left the darkened farmhouse, turning again toward her distant home. "They'll grow to hate each other yet."

Later, in the small hours of night, the farmer and his wife heard their baby crying—again. "It's your turn, wife," the farmer said sleepily.

"No, it's yours!" she shot back. So the farmer dragged himself out of bed and stumbled to the baby's room.

"Wife! Come here!" he called suddenly. When his wife rushed in, she saw him standing by the cradle with the baby in his arms. The little creature was sleeping peacefully. And what a beautiful face!

"He stopped crying when I picked him up! Is this our child?" the farmer asked, bewildered.

They took a long look at the soft smooth skin, the round little head, the wispy fair hair, the dimpled cheek. The farm wife glanced at the open window. Then she turned to her husband. "All I know . . . is that this is our baby!" she said, her face luminous with joy.

And the next night, as the trolls under the mountain rose yawning from their nettle-covered beds, the troll-father looked at his baby and said, "Well, hag wife, he slept through most of the day—and at least he's finally growing. Getting almost as handsome as me!"

Then the entire family watched with delight as their baby gulped down three whole frogs and a handful of polliwogs for breakfast.

In a short time the human baby was sleeping regularly through the night, and the troll-baby through the day—since sooner or later babies learn to sleep when they should.

And their mothers and fathers were proud of them, and took them to church or trollfest to show them off. And everyone forgot about all the trouble they'd been, which is usually how it goes.

o if you happened to pass the farmhouse, or the open door of the troll-cave, you'd probably hear a mother or father, or sister or brother, singing a lullaby and murmuring, "Oh! You're such a *good* baby!"

To Mike, Jane, Mary, Rawley, Julie, Katie, Matt, Anne, Martha, and Mark, my dear littermates. I love you all so much—and you were such *good* babies!
—T. M.

To three little trollkins, Colin, Daniel, and Benjamin
K. M.

Text copyright © 2005 by Tim Myers
Illustrations copyright © 2005 by Kelly Murphy

First edition 2005

Library of Congress Cataloging-in-Publication Data

Myers, Tim (Tim Brian)
Good Babies / Tim Myers ; illustrated by Kelly Murphy. — 1st ed.
p. cm.
Summary: A wicked witch's plan to wreak havoc by switching a human baby and a troll baby backfires in a surprising way.
ISBN 0-7636-2227-3
[1. Babies—Fiction. 2. Trolls—Fiction. 3. Norway—Fiction.]
I. Murphy, Kelly, date, ill. II. Title.
PZ7.M9919Go 2005
2004058471

2 4 6 8 10 9 7 5 3 1

Printed in China

This book was typeset in Quercus.
The illustrations were done in acrylic, watercolor, and gel medium.

Candlewick Press
2067 Massachusetts Avenue
Cambridge, Massachusetts 02140

visit us at www.candlewick.com